Small Gifts in God's Hands

Karen Hill, my assistant, and I dedicate this book to Shelby.

Published in Nashville, Tennessee, by Tommy Nelson®, a division of Thomas Nelson, Inc.

Library of Congress Cataloging-in-Publication Data
Lucado, Max.
    Small gifts in God's hands / by Max Lucado; illustrated by Cheri Bladholm.
      p. cm.
    Summary: A young boy named Elijah learns that no gift is too small in God's hands as
he watches Jesus feed thousands of hungry people from Elijah's basket of bread and fish.
    ISBN 0-8499-5842-3
      1. Jesus Christ--Miracles--Juvenile fiction. 2. Feeding of the five thousand
(Miracle)--Juvenile fiction. [1. Jesus Christ--Miracles--Fiction. 2. Feeding of the five
thousand (Miracle)--Fiction.] I. Bladholm, Cheri, ill. II. Title.

PZ7.L9684 Sm 2000
[E]--dc 21   00-033945

Printed in the United States of America

00 01 02 03 04 05 BVG 9 8 7 6 5 4 3 2 1

MAX LUCADO

Small Gifts in God's Hands

Tommy
NELSON®

Thomas Nelson, Inc.
Nashville

Illustrated by **Cheri Bladholm**

"Mother, people are still coming!" Elijah said as he stood on a stool and looked out the window of their small house.

His mother, Miriam, glanced up from her work. "Is he still in the boat?"

"Yes, he's still in Uncle Peter's boat."

"And what is he doing?"

Elijah squinted into the morning sun. "He's speaking to all the people. May I go hear him?"

"Is your work done?"

"No, but if I wait, he may be gone."

"If you don't finish your chores, I will not have any bread or fish to sell. You may go after you've finished."

As Elijah headed outside to clean the oven, he said to his mother, "Some of the boys say the Teacher Jesus is from God, Mother. Is he?"

Miriam brushed back stray hairs from her forehead. Her dark eyes smiled at her ten-year-old son. "I don't know, Elijah. But if he is, he would want you to clean the oven."

The boy smiled and when he did, Miriam saw a glimpse of his father. Elijah had the same contagious smile, dimpled chin, and even his bushy eyebrows lifted the same way when he was excited. He was a good boy. She depended on his help with the chores. And right now, the oven needed cleaning.

The job was big because the oven was big. Elijah's father had built a large oven for the inn he hoped to have one day. Then came the illness and his death. Now, the big oven, a small house, and a sweet memory were all that was left for his family. But Miriam and Elijah had made the best of it.

Every day they prepared food to sell to fishermen and travelers. While Elijah cleaned the oven, his mother prepared the bread. While she baked the bread, he went to the shore to buy the fish. And while she cooked the fish, Elijah set out the baskets for the food.

They would not get rich, but neither would they go hungry.

"Elijah! Elijah!" It was Aaron, Elijah's cousin and best friend.

Elijah raised up so quickly, he bumped his head on the oven. "Aaron, you scared me."

"Come see what the Teacher Jesus did! My father's boat is so full of fish it's almost sinking! None of the fishermen caught anything all night. The Teacher convinced them to try again, and now Father's boat and another boat are overflowing with fish."

Elijah looked toward his mother. She was standing in the doorway, holding a basket—the one he used to carry fish from the shore. She handed him the basket, smiling her approval, and the two boys were off and running.

Within moments, the two boys were in the thick of the crowd, elbowing their way to where the boats had pulled ashore. Just as Aaron had said, the boats were so full that fish were tumbling over the sides and splashing back into the water. Aaron's father, Peter, was talking loudly and gesturing wildly.

The Teacher Jesus was sitting on the edge of the boat, feet in the sand, smiling. He seemed to be enjoying the moment. Every so often he would chuckle and shake his head at Peter's description. It was after one such chuckle that his eyes met those of Elijah.

Elijah gathered up some of the fish and hurried home to tell his mother what the Teacher had done. She laughed at his imitation of Peter's excitement.

"Mother, the Teacher looked at me." Elijah stopped and thought for a moment. "You know how it feels when the morning sun chases the chill off the sea? It was like that when Jesus looked at me. I felt warm and happy."

Later that day when all their chores were done, Elijah was still talking about the fish in Peter's boat. "Mother, Uncle Peter let the Teacher use a boat. I wish we had something he could use."

He looked around at the tiny house. There wasn't much to see—the jars and cooking pots and baskets, the broom in the corner, the lamp, and the mats on the floor.

"We don't have anything big enough to give."

Miriam touched her son's cheek. "If the Teacher is who they say he is, the size of the gift doesn't matter. God can do big things with a small gift."

Elijah shrugged and sighed but said nothing.

It was a week before Elijah heard that Jesus was back in the village. This time it was Joseph, Aaron's neighbor, who came running with the news.

"He asked my father if our house could be borrowed for the afternoon. He's there right now, and so is half of Galilee."

The three hurried to Joseph's house, but there was no way they could see the Teacher. Every doorway was packed. People were sitting in the window. Four men had even gone up on the roof and lowered someone on a mat down through a hole. Joseph's father had the largest house in town, and it still couldn't hold all the people.

"I'd love for him to use our house," Elijah told his mother that night as he rolled out his bed mat. "But it wouldn't do him any good. It's too small. Everything we have is too small."

Miriam smiled and put her arm around her boy. "Remember what I said, son. If Jesus is who they say he is, he can do big things with a small gift."

The next day Elijah and Miriam went to a special meal at Peter's house. Everyone had questions about the Teacher. Peter told story after story about Jesus.

One caught Elijah's attention. It was about a woman and a jar of perfume. When she heard Jesus was in town, she went to where he was eating and poured the perfume on his feet.

While the story inspired everyone else, it discouraged young Elijah. He wanted so badly to give something to Jesus. But he had no expensive perfume. He had no house. He had no boat. He had nothing.

"Still wishing you had something big to give Jesus?" Elijah's mother asked as they were walking home.

He nodded.

"As I've said, if the Teacher is who they say he is, he doesn't need big things."

"I know, I know," Elijah interrupted. "God can do big things with a small gift."

Miriam smiled at her son. "I've been thinking," she said. "Let's get up early tomorrow and go hear what the Teacher has to say. Peter says he's not far from here."

Elijah was so excited he could hardly sleep that night for thinking about Jesus.

When Elijah awoke, the sun had yet
to appear. Careful not to disturb his
mother, he filled a basket with fish and
bread to take with them. By the time
Miriam awoke, both her son and the
food were ready to go.

Soon the two of them were climbing
the hillside with many others who
were also going to hear Jesus. It took
them a long time. Elijah had never
seen so many people. There were
thousands. Aaron had saved space for
them close to the front.

The time passed quickly as they sat on
the grass, listening to Jesus teach and
watching him heal the sick. A long line
of people waited to see the Teacher—
parents with children, people on crutches,
elderly with frail backs and weak eyes.
All wanted a moment with Jesus.

Aaron pointed to his father, Peter, in a group huddled behind Jesus. "They are worried about the size of the crowd. I heard them asking, 'How are all of these people going to eat?'"

About that time, the group of men walked toward Jesus. "You must tell the people to go home," one man said. "They are tired, and we have no food to feed them."

Jesus looked out over the crowd, and then back to the followers. "You feed them."

The men were silent. How could they feed them? What little food they had would not feed so many people.

"If only we had brought more food," Miriam said sadly. "What we have with us is so small."

Elijah smiled. He knew exactly what to do. "If Jesus is who they say he is, Mother, he can do big things with a small gift."

Elijah picked up the basket he had packed with bread and fish that morning. As he took it to one of Jesus' followers, Elijah looked at the Teacher. And when he did, Jesus looked back and smiled. Elijah didn't know what would happen, but he knew *something* would.

The follower gave the basket to Jesus. The Teacher took the food, then looked into heaven and prayed. What happened next, Elijah would never forget. It was as if the basket had no bottom. People pulled out one piece of bread after another. One fish after another. Every person on the hillside was fed, and food was left over.

At one point, as the people were eating, Elijah noticed that Jesus was looking at him. When Elijah looked back, the Teacher smiled. And when Jesus smiled, Elijah's heart felt warm and happy, the way it had the day he saw Jesus by the fishing boats.

Elijah never forgot that look. And he never forgot what he learned. He remembered both many months later as he and Aaron and Peter stood on a hill near Jerusalem. They watched from a distance as the Teacher was hung on a cross.

All three of them were very sad. "He's giving his life as a gift to save the world," his uncle said sadly.

"But he is just one life," said Aaron, "and the world is so big. How can one life save everyone? It seems like such a small gift."

Elijah squeezed his uncle's hand and smiled because he knew the answer: *No gift is small in God's hands.*